GW00858799

SAM PARROW IN TIME TO SAY GOODBYE

Sam's 7th exciting time travel adventure

Gill Parkes

Copyright © 2022 Gill Parkes

All rights reserved

The nature of this book makes the appearance of certain biblical characters and events inevitable. All other characters and events portrayed in this book are fictitious and any similarity to real persons, living or dead, is coincidental and not intended by the author.
Scripture quotations are taken from the NIV translation and used with permission.

No part of this book may be reproduced, or stored in a retrieval system, or transmitted in any form or by any means, electronic, mechanical, photocopying, recording, or otherwise, without express written permission of the publisher.

ISBN: 9798433454989
Imprint: Independently published

Cover design by: Art Painter
Library of Congress Control Number: 2018675309
Printed in the United States of America

For Mum and Dad

Because you believed, we will meet again
and what a wonderful day that will be!

*"For God loved the world so much
that he gave his only Son,
so that everyone who believes in him
may not die but have eternal life."*

John ch 3 vs 16 Good News Translation

CONTENTS

MAP OF ISRAEL

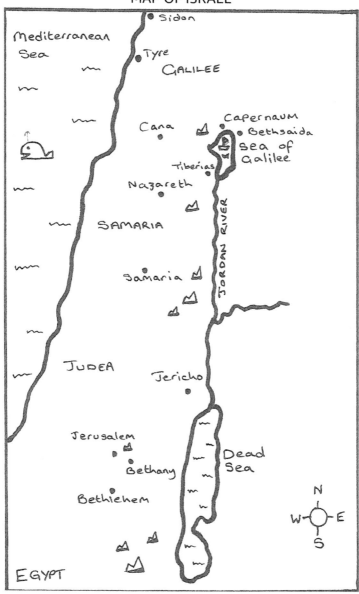

LIST OF CHARACTERS

Alex, Ben & Jamie - *Sam's friends, 21st Century*

Andy - *Sam's Dad*

Barabbas – *Criminal accused of murder*

Chris - *Youth group leader*

Crowd - *people paid to discredit Jesus*

Cupbearer/Chief Baker - *Pharaoh's servants*

Daniel - *Advisor to King Darius*

Eli & Jacob - *Rachel's brothers*

Granny & Gramps – *Sam's grandparents*

Hepzibah - *the goat*

Herod - *King at time of Jesus' birth*

Isaac - *Rachel's husband*

Jesus - *Messiah*

Jo - *Sam's Mum*

John, Judas, Peter - *Disciples of Jesus*

Joseph - *Prisoner, Interpreter of dreams*

Joseph & Mary - *Jesus' parents*

Joshua - *Leader of the Israelites after Moses*

Kate & Dayle - *Sisters, Sam's friends, 21st century*

Matthew - *Sam's friend, 1st century*

Moses - *Israelite leader*

Ollie & Jack - *Year 7 bullies*

Pharaoh - *King of Egypt*

Pilate - *Governor of Jerusalem*

Potiphar - *Captain of the Guard*

Rachel - *Sam's friend, 1st century*

Sam - *12-yr-old time traveller*

Sue - *Chris' wife*

Yahweh - *The One True God*

And various nobles, traders, guards and household slaves

CHAPTER 1

When Sam's granny broke her hip his parents were unable to take their usual summer holiday at their cottage in Norfolk. Youth Group leader Chris and his wife Sue offered to take Sam along with his friends, Alex, Jamie, Ben, Kate and her sister Dayle. One evening, while singing songs around a campfire on the beach, Sam had gone back to the cottage to phone home but instead of returning to the group, the time stone had whisked him away on another adventure.

Sam was gone for almost two years but as usual, the time stone brought him back to the time that he had left. To the rest of the group, he'd only been gone for a few minutes but when he returned to the beach, Sam was distraught and had burst into tears.

It had taken a while but he eventually managed to pour out the whole of his extraordinary story. Sam had gone right back to the beginning, telling them how the strange stone he had found during his last holiday at the cottage turned out to be a time stone that took him back in time to Bethlehem. There he had joined Rachel and the shepherds who had witnessed Jesus' birth. Since then he had been on many adventures to see events written about in the bible, both before and after that time.

To say that the others were surprised was an understatement. Chris, Sue, Dayle, Jamie and Ben had all been sceptical at first but when Alex and Kate had joined in to share their stories of how they had occasionally accompanied Sam they had reluctantly believed him. Chris shook his head and looked at him in astonishment.

"No wonder you asked so many interesting questions!" he said.

"Yeah, I've learnt so much but every trip gives me more stuff to ask about!"

Sam pulled the blanket that Sue had given him more tightly around his shoulders. The after-effects of travelling through time had worn off but the events that happened before his return were making him shiver. His last trip had been the long-est and most difficult with Sam having to work as a slave in Potiphar's kitchen. Unfortunately, his arch-enemy Ollie Jones had gone back with him but had been left behind, shut away in prison with Joseph.

"You've really been away for two years?" asked Kate. Sam nodded miserably.

"You don't look older, you haven't even grown!" said Ben who was still having trouble coming to terms with the idea of Sam travelling back in time and experiencing everything he had spoken about. It wasn't helping with his feelings of jeal-ousy towards Sam either, it just made him feel more left out than ever. It did explain why Sam and Kate were getting on so well though, which was another thing he didn't like. He'd been trying to get to know Kate long before Sam came on the scene!

"I had grown, they had to give me another tunic because my old one didn't fit anymore. I'd even got some muscle from baking bread! I always come back to the same point that I left though and everything returns to how it was then." Sam smiled, "The first time I was away for a few months was on the ark and my hair grew so long

I was worried Mum would freak out when she saw me. When I looked in the mirror though it was just how it always is."

The three boys looked incredulous as they tried to imagine Sam taller and stronger. The girls just grinned, Sam was the smallest boy in school, trying to picture him any differently was beyond them!

"So what happens now?" asked Jamie, "I mean, you can't leave Ollie in prison, even if he does deserve to be there." Sam sighed.

"I know but I can only go back to the time and place the time stone decides to take me."

"Surely if this is God's doing he knows exactly what has happened," said Chris, "Maybe we should leave it up to him to sort out."

"I agree," said Sue, "Right now you need hot chocolate and sleep. I suggest we all pray for wisdom and peace and leave it in his capable hands. We can talk again in the morning."

Snuggling down into his sleeping bag, Sam sighed. He had no idea what was going to happen next, he had to trust that Chris was right and that God knew what he was doing. They would just have to wait until God allowed Ollie to come back to where he belonged.

The next day was hot again but with a slight breeze coming off the sea to keep them cool they all agreed to spend another day on the beach. Chris carried on teaching the others to surf while Sam spent some much needed time alone on his board. After two years working as a kitchen slave, he was having trouble getting used to life in the twenty-first century. His outer appearance might have returned to normal but how he felt on the inside was very different.

Lying on his back with the waves gently rolling beneath his board, he looked up at the clear blue sky. He remembered the words that Daniel had said when he was faced with being thrown to the lions. He had spoken about trusting God and giving thanks despite our circumstances, even when things looked bad. We might not know how everything would turn out but God did. He cared about us and he would not let us down. Sam decided it was time to follow Daniel's example.

"Thank you, Yahweh, for looking after me and bringing me home safely," he prayed, "I know that there is a reason for all of this and that you love Ollie, even though he can be mean. Please keep him safe and help him to learn about you just as I have. You have given me some amazing friends and changed my life completely. Thank you, I think you are awesome."

A gentle breeze blew over Sam and as he turned over to paddle back to shore he felt at peace knowing that God had heard his prayer and that all would be well when the time was right.

For the rest of the afternoon, Ben kept a close eye on Sam in the hope of seeing him disappear but the time stone remained silent and Sam stayed put.

After dinner, that evening, time travel and Ollie were temporarily forgotten as they tried to outdo each other with a hilarious game of charades. Eventually though, it was time for bed and the boys made their way to the tent that was tucked in between the cottage and the dunes. Jamie and Alex very quickly settled down to sleep, tired from the day's activities. Both found surfing hard work, although they had spent more time on the board this time, unlike the day before when they had spent most of the time falling off into the sea.

Ben, however, was restless. Even though he had

felt included while they played games, his feelings towards Sam were beginning to get the better of him again. Hearing a noise, he opened the flap to the room he shared with Jamie and saw Sam making his way outside. As quietly as he could so as not to disturb the others, Ben eased himself out of his sleeping bag and followed. Sam was sitting just outside the tent, looking up at the stars. Ben joined him and sat hugging his knees.

"I can't sleep either," he sighed. Sam smiled and pointed up at the sky.

"There's the plough," he said, "It's good to know that the sky has stayed the same even though everything in the world has changed. It makes me feel safe somehow."

"Safe?"

"Yeah. It sort of makes you realise that God's still the same too and he's been around even longer than the stars have!"

Just then a low hum came from the pocket in Sam's hoody.

"What's that noise?" asked Ben. Sam grinned.

"Time to leave!" he said, as he held the stone in one hand and Ben in the other.

CHAPTER 2

Even though Sam had told them what it was like, travelling through time still came as a shock to Ben. He sat still, taking deep breaths to try to clear the nausea and dizziness, and fervently wished the world would stop spinning. Sam looked on in sympathy.

"Don't worry, it doesn't last long, I hardly feel it at all now." Putting the time stone away in his leather pouch, Sam explained that they were just outside Bethlehem where he usually met Rachel. He looked around for her and was surprised to see there were more sheep than before. There seemed to be more shepherds too but he couldn't see Rachel anywhere.

"Come on, we'll go and look for her, she can't be far away. Oh, and I need to explain some of the words they use." Sam started towards the camp, giving Ben a lesson in what to do and say so that he didn't appear strange. As they got closer, Sam recognised Rachel's older brother Eli among the group of men sitting around the fire. He didn't know how long he had been away but hoped that Eli hadn't forgotten him.

"Shalom!" Sam called as he approached the camp. Eli looked up.

"Shalom! Is that Samuel, Rachel's young friend?"

"Yes and this is Benjamin."

"You look no different to when you were here a year ago! Come sit with us. Rachel will be here soon with our supper."

Eli returned to his conversation, leaving Sam to think about the length of time he had been away. He wondered if Rachel had changed much since he had last seen her. It wasn't long before they heard singing coming from the direction of the town. Sam smiled, he would recognise that voice any-where! As she got closer, Sam could see that Rachel was taller and wore a veil over her hair. Her tunic was ankle-length, unlike the short one she had worn at his last visit. Rachel was no longer the girl he had left behind, she was growing into a lovely young woman. Sam gulped, he hoped it was only her appearance that had changed!

Rachel gave Eli the food that she had brought

and smiled shyly at the young man sitting next to him. Eli shook his head and frowned.

"Rachel, your friend Samuel is here. You should go and speak with him," he said sternly.

Startled, Rachel turned to look in the direction that Eli nodded.

"Oh, my goodness!" she said, "I didn't know you had returned." Immediately she went over to where Sam and Ben were sitting, slightly apart from the rest of the group. "Come, help me fill the water jar at the stream."

Leading the boys away to where they couldn't be overheard, Rachel let out a squeal and enveloped Sam in a hug. He laughed as he realised she hadn't changed at all!

"Eli said I've been away a year!"

"More than that, you left just before my thirteenth birthday. I'm fourteen now." She smiled, "And who is this?"

"Oh, this is Ben. I told you about him the last time I was here."

"Shalom, Ben. It is good to meet a friend of Sam's."

"Er, shalom," Ben stammered, hoping that was the right thing to say.

Sam grinned, "I wasn't sure what to say to you

when I saw you. You look so grown up! And where is Jacob? I'm surprised he's not here with this many sheep to look after!"

"Oh Sam, so much has happened this year. Abba finally found an honest wool merchant to apprentice Jacob to so he has left us to live in Jerusalem."

"Oh wow, that's exactly what he wanted! He must be a lot happier now."

"Yes, I think so although we don't see him very often. I'm sure he will return though once his apprenticeship is finished."

Sam didn't say anything, he knew from meeting Rachel again when she was much older that Jacob would eventually marry and make his home in Jerusalem. He asked instead about the new shepherds that were sitting with Eli around the fire. Rachel blushed.

"The one sat next to Eli is called Isaac, the other two are his brothers," she said, "Our Abbas have been discussing marriage. We are to be betrothed soon."

Ben gasped, "But you're so young!" he said. Rachel smiled kindly, she understood from her conversations with Sam that life was very different for the two boys.

"Things are done differently here, Ben. It is not

unusual for girls to be married at my age although boys tend to be a little older."

Sam was not at all surprised as he knew that Rachel got married when she was sixteen. He also knew he would be going to the wedding and would have to tell her that it would be the last time he saw her until she was much older.

"Is that why Eli sent you away tonight?" he asked. Rachel grinned.

"Yes, we're not supposed to be with each other until we are betrothed and only then if we have a chaperone."

"Really? How do you get to know each other then?" Ben shook his head finding it hard to believe just how different life was in first-century Israel.

Rachel filled her jar at the stream then turned to walk back to the camp, "We trust our parents to make a good match, we have many years ahead of us to get to know each other." Turning to Sam she said, "Tell me what has happened since I last saw you. Has the time stone taken you anywhere?"

Sam rolled his eyes, "I've been a slave in Egypt for two years!" he groaned.

"Two years! When? What were you doing?" she asked looking aghast and wondering how he had managed for so long without her. She hoped he had found another friend to help him.

"I was with Joseph. He helped me a lot but then he was put in prison. The thing is, Ollie had gone with me and he ended up in prison too!"

"The boy who fought with you?"

"Yes, only he didn't come back. He's still there!"

"Oh my goodness!" Rachel stood still and put the jar of water down on the grass. "How will he get home?"

"I don't know. I guess we have to wait for the time stone to take me back again!"

Right on cue, the stone made its presence known as it began to hum.

CHAPTER 3

The three friends found themselves on the edge of a huge camp of people.

"I'm guessing this isn't Egypt," said Ben, looking around at the vast crowd that seemed to stretch for miles.

"No, it reminds me of when we joined the exodus," said Sam.

"Mmm, I wonder if it still is? Let's see if we can find Moses," Rachel made her way through the camp, listening in on conversations to try to work out when they had arrived. As they walked past women preparing food, Sam frowned and pulled Rachel aside.

"It can't be the exodus," he said, "There's no manna or quail. I thought that was all they ate until they reached the land Yahweh had promised them."

"Yes, you're right, but there's so many of them!" Rachel puzzled over where they could be when they saw a man leave the camp and walk towards the city that was a little way off. "Come on, let's follow him."

The three friends hurried to catch up with the man, staying far enough back for him not to notice. When he got nearer the city walls he stopped. The children crept nearer and hid themselves behind a large rock. Suddenly, a man holding a sword appeared in front of him.

"Wow, where did he come from?" gasped Ben.

"Shh!" whispered the others in unison. They watched as the man they had been following went up to him and said,

"Are you for us or for our enemies?"

"Neither," replied the man with the sword, "but as commander of the army of the Lord I have now come." The first man fell face down to the ground and asked,

"What message does my Lord have for his servant?" In reply, the Commander told him to remove his sandals as he was standing on holy ground. Then he said,

"I have given Jericho to you, along with its king and its fighting men. Once a day for six days you must march around the city with your army. In front of them, seven priests should carry trumpets of ram's horns before the ark. On the seventh day, march around the city seven times with the priests blowing the trumpets. When the priests sound a long blast, make all the people give a loud shout. Then the walls will collapse and you should go in and take the city."

The man returned to the camp while the children remained hidden, stunned by what they had heard.

"Joshua!" exclaimed Rachel, "and the city is Jericho!"

"So this is the promised land," declared Sam, "That's why they were eating normal food."

"Do you think we'll get to see the walls fall down?" asked Ben. Sam grinned,

"I hope so!" he said, "That would be awesome!"

Just then the time stone began to hum. Ben looked disappointed.

"Oh, are we going home already?" he asked.

"Maybe not, sometimes we just move forward a couple of days," replied Sam reaching into his pouch for the stone, "Hold on!" A flash of blue light lit up the area where they were but when they opened their eyes again it seemed that everything was exactly the same as the place they had left.

The only difference was the time of day; it was just beginning to get light.

"I wonder how many days have gone by?" said Rachel, looking towards the camp, "Look! They're coming!"

The children watched as Joshua's army marched behind the trumpeters and the ark which held the stone tablets given to Moses on Mount Sinai. Yahweh himself had written the Ten Commandments on them and the people believed they were sacred. They knew that if the ark was leading the army, Yahweh was leading them too.

No one spoke a word, the only sounds came from hundreds of marching feet and the blast of the trumpets carried by the priests. Led by the trumpeters, the army marched silently around the walls of the city. Having gone around once, instead of going back to camp, the priests led the way around again.

"It's the last day," whispered Rachel excitedly. She was right; the army marched around seven times before coming to a halt in front of the city gates. It was incredibly eerie watching them, this huge army marching in silence. Sam gulped, it must be terrifying to be inside the city, not knowing what was going on.

Suddenly, the trumpeters sounded a long blast and the people gave a huge shout. With a mighty roar, the walls collapsed and the army rushed inside to take the city. In all the commotion no one noticed the three children who had come out from behind the rock to watch the fall of Jericho. Nor did they notice the strange blue light which took them back to Bethlehem.

CHAPTER 4

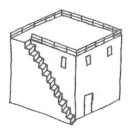

"Oh wow," said Ben, "That was awesome!"

Sam grinned, "Glad you came?"

"Totally!"

Rachel smiled, she'd missed her adventures with Sam. Seeing the stories she had been taught happening in real life made Yahweh seem much closer, especially now that everything was changing for her.

"I need to take this water back to camp," she said. "Will you come?"

Sam hesitated, he would have much preferred to talk to Rachel alone. This was the first time he had shared her with anyone and he began to realise how Ben must have been feeling about his friendship with Kate. He knew though that they could only leave when the time stone took them.

"We'll stay until the time stone decides otherwise!" he said.

The three friends walked back to the shepherds' camp, lost in their own thoughts about the events they had just seen.

"I wonder who the commander of the Lord's army was?" said Ben.

Rachel shrugged, "An angel I suppose." Sam just nodded, he wasn't sure, it was a question he needed to ask Chris. As they got close to the camp the stone began to hum.

"Time to go, Ben," said Sam as he reached for the stone. Rachel smiled and waving goodbye she carried on to where Eli and Isaac were waiting for her.

The two boys were standing outside a house in the town. Sam recognised it as the one he visited in the future when Rachel was older. Sounds of music and laughter were coming from the garden.

"Our clothes are different!" exclaimed Ben as he looked at the colourful coat he wore over his tunic.

"I think this must be Rachel's wedding," Sam sighed, he wasn't looking forward to saying goodbye, even though he knew it wouldn't be forever.

Opening the gate, Sam led the way into the garden where tables were set out around the edge.

In the centre, a group of men were dancing, just as they had been at the first wedding Sam had been to in Cana. That had been the time when the wine had run out and Jesus had made more from jars filled with water. He grinned, it had been great fun joining in with the dancing and singing. Sam looked over at the table positioned beneath a decorated canopy. Rachel was sat surrounded by her friends and looked beautiful in her wedding clothes. When she noticed Sam, she smiled shyly and beckoned him over to the table.

"I'm so glad you've come, I was hoping you would. I even asked Yahweh if I could see you one more time!"

Sam grinned, "I couldn't miss this!" he said, "It looks like a great party."

"It's good that Ben is here with you so you are not alone."

"Yes, we've just left you after going to Jericho."

Rachel frowned, puzzled by the way the time stone worked. Shaking her head she decided that it wasn't important, she was just glad that her friend from the future had been able to join in with the best day of her life.

"You must join in the dancing!" she laughed, clapping her hands in delight as Jacob came over to greet the boys. He shook his head in amazement.

"Samuel, you look no different to when I saw you three years ago! Do you never grow? Come and join us, your playmate has become a woman today!"

Jacob pulled Sam into the circle while Ben watched from the side. He was astonished at how well Sam fitted in. He even knew the steps to the dances! It made him realise that everything Sam had told them about his trips into the past was true. After watching for a short time he felt confident enough to join in so when someone grabbed his arm and pulled him into the circle Ben laughed and happily joined the dance.

Eventually, the music stopped so that they could get their breath and enjoy the delicious food that was laid out on the tables. While they were eating, Rachel came over to speak to them.

"Are you having fun?" she asked, "You danced much better than I would have expected!"

Sam grinned, "Yes, this isn't the first wedding I've been to here!"

Rachel frowned, "Oh, did you attend one when you were in Egypt? I wouldn't have thought slaves would be allowed to join in."

Sam took a deep breath, knowing that this was the opportunity he had been waiting for.

"No, it was at your cousin's wedding in your future. This is the last time I see you until you are much older."

Rachel sighed, she had been expecting this but had hoped it wouldn't be for some time yet.

"We will meet again?" she asked.

"Yes, when your youngest son is the age I am now."

Rachel squealed and clapped her hands, she was sad that Sam wouldn't return for many years but she was excited to know that she would have a son!

"I will have a baby boy?" she asked. Sam laughed,

"Two boys and two girls!" he said, forgetting that he wasn't supposed to reveal anything that happens in the future. Oh well maybe, just this once, it wouldn't matter. Rachel laughed and hugged Sam for the last time.

"And will you look as you do now?" she asked.

"Exactly the same as when I saw you the first time!"

Rachel nodded, smiling sadly, "I shall miss you but I look forward to seeing you again."

Rachel returned to her table under the wedding canopy where Isaac, her new husband, was waiting for her. Sam and Ben strolled around the garden, occasionally helping themselves to more food. When they reached the gate, the time stone began to hum.

"Time to go home," said Sam, glancing back for a last look at Rachel who was laughing at something Isaac had said. The boys slipped through the gate to make sure that no one saw them leave as the time stone glowed and whisked them back to their tent in the twenty-first century.

Ben looked at Sam and smiled.

"Thank you for taking me with you," he said.

"Yeah, I'm glad you came, it made it easier to say goodbye."

Ben nodded, he understood. Rachel had been a special friend to Sam and he would miss her. He yawned.

"Gosh, I'm tired!"

Sam laughed, "It's all that dancing! Come on let's go to bed. We can tell everyone about it tomorrow!"

CHAPTER 5

Over breakfast the next morning, the two boys told the others about their adventure the night before. Ben laughed as he described Sam's expertise on the dance floor.

"You would have thought he had lived there his whole life!" he said. He had been thrilled to be included in Sam's trip to Bethlehem and was feeling a lot happier about being a part of the group. Ben knew now that his feelings of jealousy were unfounded and probably came from his problems at home.

"I have a question for you, Chris," said Sam, spreading honey on another slice of toast. Really, considering how much he ate, it was a wonder Sam was as small as he was.

"Why am I not surprised?" laughed Chris, who had once said that asking questions was Sam's speciality. Sam grinned, he knew Chris didn't mind and now he knew the reason for them he probably expected to be asked a whole lot more!

"Rachel thought that the Commander of the Lord's army was an angel but I'm not sure."

"Well, you are not the only one to question that," Chris said, reaching for his bible. "Who do you think he is?"

"I don't know, I wondered if he was Jesus."

Chris nodded, "Many people think he was the archangel, Michael, who fought against Satan and threw him out of heaven. He is written about in the book of Daniel and also in Revelation, the last book of the bible."

"But what of the others, who don't think that? Who do they think he is?"

"Well, Revelation chapter nineteen tells us about the time when Jesus will come back with heaven's armies to finally put an end to Satan's rule and take back what is rightfully his. The description of the leader on the white horse could only really be Jesus."

Sam nodded, "Rachel doesn't know anything about Jesus when she's young, that's why I didn't want to say anything."

"From the stories you've told us I'm sure Rachel will find out all she needs to know in time. But when the Commander spoke to Joshua, he told him that he was standing on holy ground and didn't tell him off when he fell down in worship. That was similar to when God spoke from the burning bush when he told Moses he was to lead the Israelites out of Egypt. The very first commandment tells us that we must only ever worship God and none of the angels that appear to people in the bible say anything like what was said to Joshua. In fact, the angel that appeared to John actually told him off for kneeling in front of him! He told John that he was as much a servant of God as he was."

"So who do you think he was then?" asked Ben, intrigued by the thought that he may actually have seen Jesus in person.

"I don't think that it matters who he was. The important thing was that Joshua was told what was about to happen and what he needed to do to prepare for it. Then Joshua went back to the camp and obeyed the instructions."

"It was eerie watching them march around the walls in silence," said Sam, remembering how he had felt.

"The noise was incredible though when the walls fell down," joined in Ben.

"I bet it was!" Alex shook his head at the thought

of walls crumbling to dust just because an army had shouted at them. "Do you think they wouldn't have fallen if Joshua had tried to attack them instead?"

"Oh yes," agreed Chris, "The whole point in all of this is our obedience. God will always help us when we need him to but we have to do things his way, not ours. That way it's God who gets the glory, not us."

Sue stood up and began to clear the table.

"Come on, the sun is shining and I have a book to read while you lot wear yourselves out on your surfboards!"

They all laughed and helped Sue with the dishes before getting ready for another day on the beach.

CHAPTER 6

Later that evening, the conversation turned to Ollie and the problem of getting him back home. They all agreed that there was nothing they could do except pray and wait for God to reveal his plan.

"I wonder if he'll have changed," mused Kate, "It can't be much fun in prison."

"I'm hoping that Joseph has been able to talk to him but I suppose that will only help if Ollie listens," replied Sam, "He didn't want to when I was there."

Sue and Dayle handed round mugs of hot chocolate and a plate of biscuits, which very quickly became nothing more than a plate of crumbs.

"Maybe when Joseph is finally let out he'll be able to get Ollie out too," suggested Alex.

Sam shrugged, "Maybe. How long was Joseph in prison for anyway?"

"No one knows for sure," replied Chris, "but the general thinking is about eight to ten years."

Sam's eyes nearly popped out of his head. "That would make Ollie over twenty!" he said.

Kate looked horrified, "I think I'd die if I was in prison that long!"

"You don't think he will do you?" gasped Sam, terrified of what would happen if Ollie never came back.

"No, Sam, God has it all in hand. You mustn't worry, he won't let you down." Sue took Sam's empty mug, "I'm sure there will be a point when Ollie realises his mistakes and asks God for help. Most people turn to him when there's nowhere else to go."

Sam nodded, grateful for the support from his friends. Yawning, he stood up and stretched.

"Time for bed," he said, "You three coming?" Sam asked as he headed towards the bathroom. The others nodded and after taking turns to clean their teeth the four boys went out into the garden to settle down for another night in the tent.

Thankfully, the weather was still warm and dry so they left the tent flap open to look at the stars. Eventually, the tent grew quiet as Jamie, Ben and Alex drifted off to sleep. Sam was just about to do the same when he noticed one star seemed to be glowing brighter than the others, lighting up the garden. Curiosity driving away sleep, he eased himself out of his sleeping bag to go outside for a better look. It was while he was wondering about the significance of the star that the time stone hummed and took him back to Bethlehem.

Rachel was walking across the field towards the town and as soon as she saw Sam, she lifted her tunic and ran.

"Sam! I thought you were going home. Where's Ben?"

"Shalom! I've been home and come back again! Did I just leave you?"

"Yes, I'm on my way home."

The two friends laughed. Sam sent up a silent prayer of thanks that Yahweh had allowed him to see Rachel alone, probably for the last time. As they joined the road that would take them through the gate, the time stone hummed and flashed its blue light.

They had arrived in the outer court of the temple in Jerusalem. It was very busy and seemed more like a marketplace than a place of worship. There were people everywhere, and the noise of business mingled with the noise from the animals being sold for sacrifice.

Rachel noticed a young couple enter the court carrying a child. She smiled, she hoped that would be herself and Isaac one day. She drew Sam closer to them so that she could admire the baby and whisper congratulations to his mother. An elderly man approached the couple and took the child in his arms. Raising him up, he praised God saying,

"With my own eyes I have seen your salvation, which you have prepared in the presence of all peoples: A light to reveal your will to the Gentiles and bring glory to your people Israel."

Then he returned the child to his mother and blessed them, saying that he would grow up to cause the rise and fall of many whose hearts would be revealed by him. He also warned the woman that a sword would pierce her soul. When he had finished speaking a woman who was very old came up and spoke of all the wonderful things Yahweh had planned for the child she proclaimed to be the Messiah.

Rachel gasped, "It's Jesus! I thought he had been killed!"

Sam looked at her curiously, "No, they escaped," he said, surprised that he knew something that Rachel didn't. Just then, the time stone hummed and took them back to Bethlehem.

The two friends sat down on the grass beside the road. Rachel frowned and shook her head.

"King Herod learned that a new king had been born so he sent his soldiers to murder all the baby boys in the area. It was a terrible time, their mothers were heartbroken." A tear trickled down Rachel's cheek. At the time she had been frightened by the violence but it was only now that she was older that she realised how awful it must have been for the parents. Seeing that she was upset, Sam put his arm around her to try to comfort her.

"Our stories tell us that Joseph was warned in a dream. They escaped to Egypt where they stayed until Herod died. Then an angel told them it was safe to return and they went to live in Nazareth."

"So it's true? He really is the Messiah?"

"Yes, although I think he's different to what people expect."

Rachel nodded, she understood that because people couldn't agree on what they wanted the Messiah to do. Some wanted a warrior who would fight against the Romans, others wanted a king who would provide food and shelter and still others hoped for a miracle worker who would heal the sick. She smiled at Sam,

"Thank you for telling me that. I think perhaps you have learnt a lot from your visits to Bethlehem."

"Much more than you know," Sam agreed, "I have enjoyed coming here. I'll miss my visits when they stop."

Rachel sighed. However much she hoped that Sam would keep coming, she knew that her life was about to change forever. She had other things to think about now, someone else that she needed to get to know and start a new life with. The two friends stood up and gave each other a final hug. Of course, it was possible they would meet again, who knew what Yahweh and the time stone had planned?

As the time stone took Sam back to the twenty-first century, Rachel watched him disappear with a sad smile, knowing deep down that he wouldn't be coming back. Turning towards her home, she smoothed her tunic and straightened her veil. She was no longer a child, she was a young woman about to be married. What could be more exciting than that!

Many years in the future, in a land far to the north of Israel, the star that had shone so brightly was now just a faint glow in the sky. Sam yawned and went back into the tent where he snuggled down in his sleeping bag. As soon as his head touched his pillow, he was fast asleep.

CHAPTER 7

The next day was dry but cloudy so they decided to walk along the beach to where Sam had found the time stone. He told them all about the problems with erosion, how the coast was gradually being washed away by the sea. They could see the remains of buildings that had fallen when storms had caused the cliffs to crumble after high tides had washed away the sand and soil at the bottom. Chris said it reminded him of the parable about the house built on the sand.

"Jesus taught that people who hear his words and put them into practise are like those who build their house on the rock. They have a good foundation that will be strong when the storms of life come along. But those who hear his words and ignore them are like those who build their house on sand. The foundations are weak and will give way when the storms come. Just as the house comes crashing down, those who don't listen will find that their lives could fall apart too."

"But what about the people who never hear the things that Jesus said?" asked Jamie, "People don't go to church anymore, they think it's boring or just for old people."

Which is why we have to be different," said Sue, "If we live the way that Jesus wants us to live people will notice. Then hopefully they'll ask questions and we can tell them how much Jesus loves them."

"Yeah, it's much better to show them first," agreed Dayle, "Otherwise they just think you're preaching and shut their ears."

Sam nodded, "Alex had been asking me to go to Youth Group for ages but I thought it was just for the God Squad! It wasn't until I went along that I realised what great friends you all were."

Ben blushed, "Well, some of us," he muttered.

"No, all of you, I understand now how you felt and I'm sorry I made you feel that way." Sam grinned, "Come on, I'll race you back. I'm starving!"

Sam turned round and raced back along the

beach towards the cottage. His four friends chased after him, overtaking him just before they reached the path that would take them home over the dunes. Chris, Sue and Dayle followed at a leisurely pace, pleased that the five friends seemed to have put their differences aside. The last thing they wanted was more trouble between them.

After lunch, the sun was still failing to make an appearance so Sam dug out his cricket bat and football. Even Sue put her book aside and joined in the games that followed. Stopping for a breather, Sam turned to Chris to ask something he had been puzzling over.

"Last night Rachel and I went to the temple in Jerusalem and we saw Mary and Joseph with baby Jesus. Two old people came up, a man and a woman, and they said stuff about him."

"Oh, they would have been Simeon and Anna, they are written about in Luke's gospel. They were prophets, people who hear God speak to them and then proclaim what he said to the people."

"But what did Simeon mean when he said that people would rise and fall and that a sword would pierce Mary's soul? How is that possible?"

"Simeon was speaking about the things that Jesus would teach and how they would show people up for what they were really like. Those with good hearts would accept his teachings, even if they didn't accept him but those people who only cared for themselves and their reputations wouldn't accept anything. Simeon didn't know the details of how Jesus would live and die, but he did know that Mary's heart would break for her son. Jesus died the most painful death imaginable and his mother was there to see it. Just think how your mum would feel if she saw you suffer."

Sam shuddered, he hoped that would never happen. Then he remembered that there was another mum whose heart would break if she knew her son was in prison in ancient Egypt with no means of coming home. He sighed, he really hoped that God would do something soon. Thinking about his mum, Sam realised he hadn't spoken to her since the time stone had taken him to Egypt. Although it had only been a couple of days in his present time zone, it had been over two years if he included the time he'd spent as a slave. Explaining to Chris that he was going back to the cottage to ring his mum, Sam climbed the path over the dunes. When he reached the other side, out of sight from his friends, the time stone hummed and took Sam back in time.

CHAPTER 8

It was with great relief that Sam realised he was back in Potiphar's kitchen in ancient Egypt at exactly the same time that he had left. He watched the guards drag Ollie off to prison then returned to work, no longer worried that Ollie would be left behind. Sam trusted God to do whatever was necessary to get him back to where he belonged.

Having finished his work for the day, Sam went to his room. After Joseph had been promoted all the slaves were given better accommodation and Ollie and Sam had shared a room just big enough for their two mattresses with a small space for their meagre belongings. It had once been a storeroom, but Joseph's success meant that bigger storerooms had needed to be built, freeing up extra space for the slaves. As long as they did their work and didn't cause trouble the slaves were treated well.

Sam wondered what would happen, now that

both Ollie and Joseph were in prison. When he had gone home after the first time he had seen Joseph, Sam had read his story in Genesis, the first book of the bible. Unfortunately, like in so many of them, a lot of details had been missed out and he had no idea how long he would have to wait for things to happen. He supposed he would just have to carry on working as he had before until God decided it was time for him to leave.

Another year passed and Sam had grown into a fine young man. He was no longer the little kid that had arrived three years before. Lifting heavy trays in and out of the oven and kneading bread had made him stronger. It hadn't been easy to keep track of the date but Sam had an idea that it was somewhere around his sixteenth birthday. He was now an accomplished baker and was given a lot more responsibility in the kitchen. Although he missed his family and friends in the twenty-first century, he had made friends with some of the other slaves and was well-liked by those in charge of the kitchen. Sam knew he wouldn't be there for-ever but until it was time to leave he was going to make the best of it.

Early one morning, Sam arrived in the kitchen ready to start work and found the chief baker red-faced and muttering angrily as he mixed the dough for the day's bread.

"What's wrong?" he asked, dodging out of the way when the baker threw the dough onto the board and started kneading it ferociously.

"The chief baker to the king has been put into our prison! Because of his stupidity, I have been told to send my best assistant to the palace to help them in his place."

Sam frowned, wondering who would be leaving to go to work in the palace. It wasn't long before his question was answered.

"Samuel, you are to leave as soon as you have collected your belongings. In the meantime, I must continue to bake bread for Potiphar's house-hold alone. How can I be expected to feed all these people without help! Go, before I change my mind and upset the king by keeping you here."

Sam stood rooted to the spot, amazed that the chief baker considered him to be his best assistant. He was going to bake for the king! Sam wasn't sure if he should feel thrilled that he was good enough or terrified in case he made a mistake. Quickly, Sam left the kitchen and went to collect the few belongings he had acquired in the last three years of being a slave. Just as he was about to leave, Sam noticed a low hum coming from the pouch fastened to his belt. He gulped, he hoped the baker wouldn't get into trouble when Sam didn't turn up at the palace.

Sam blinked and tried to see where he was but it was too dark. The only sounds were the squeaks and patter of creatures that shared his space and a gentle snore that came from close by. Being careful not to disturb whoever else was there, Sam stretched out his hands to feel the ground around him. Wherever he was, it was cold and damp. Something ran across his foot and Sam gasped, biting his lip so that he didn't shout out. He had an idea where the stone had brought him to but he needed a bit more light to be sure.

After a while a tiny window high up in the wall allowed the daylight to filter through. It wasn't much, just enough for Sam to see that he was in a small cell with one other occupant. A bucket sat in the corner and from the smell, Sam guessed it was the toilet. On the thin mattress next to him he saw a young man, about the same age. He looked weak and unkempt and smelt like he hadn't washed for some time. Tears trickled down Sam's face as he realised that prison had not been kind to Ollie.

Waking up, Ollie stretched and yawned. Rubbing his eyes, he gave a start when he saw Sam sitting on the floor.

"I didn't hear them bring anyone in," he grumbled, unhappy at having to share his small space, "Who are you? What did you do?"

"Ollie, I'm Sam. The time stone brought me."

"Sam? You can't be, you're too big, he's just a kid."

"Yeah, but it's been two years since we came to Egypt and another year since you were put in here. I've grown up."

"Huh! I suppose you've been enjoying yourself while I've been cooped up here starving every day."

"Yes actually, I have. But I've also worked hard and been concerned about you."

"Seriously? I bet you were glad to be rid of me!"

Ollie was feeling sorry for himself and wasn't bothered about Sam knowing it. Just then they heard noises coming from the end of the corridor.

"That will be Joseph. He acts like he's the warder even though he's a prisoner too. Loser! You wouldn't catch me emptying the buckets!"

Sam shook his head, couldn't Ollie see it would be better for him if he could learn from Joseph? Just then the time stone began to hum.

"Finally! Give it to me! Let's see how you like being here instead," Ollie lunged at Sam to try to snatch the stone off him but he was no longer a match for him. Sam held on tightly to the stone which whisked them both forward in time.

CHAPTER 9

Ollie had hoped the stone would take them home but all it did was move them to a different cell. This one was bigger and already had two occupants, neither of whom seemed very happy. The cell was dark enough and big enough for them not to notice the two boys who had just arrived. Sam warned Ollie to be quiet and listen. From the conversation between the two men, Sam learned that they were the king's cupbearer and chief baker and had been in prison for a long time. While asleep a few nights before, both men had dreams that had frightened them. Joseph had told the men that Yahweh had spoken to them through their dreams about what was to happen to them.

"What did I do that was so bad?" grumbled the chief baker, "I don't deserve to die!"

"Maybe Joseph got it wrong," murmured the

cupbearer trying to comfort his friend, "Perhaps the dream has another meaning and you will be released with me."

"But if he was wrong about my dream, he could have been wrong about yours!"

The cupbearer sighed, for his own sake he hoped that Joseph was right but it wasn't looking good for the chief baker. Just then, the prison guard came and unlocked the cell.

"It's your lucky day!" he said to the two men who were sat shaking nervously, "It's Pharaoh's birthday and he has requested your presence. Get moving!"

The guard pulled them up roughly and led them out before locking the door behind him. As he did so, the time stone hummed and whisked Sam and Ollie to the palace. Ollie was about to dash off but Sam held on to him to stop him from escaping.

"If you leave now you may never get home!" he hissed. Reluctantly, Ollie crouched with Sam behind a pillar to watch the proceedings. Sam's eyes began to water, Ollie really did need a bath!

Pharaoh, the king of Egypt, called for the cupbearer and chief baker to be brought to him. In front of all his officials, he pardoned the cupbearer and restored him to his previous position. Everyone applauded his good fortune and the cupbearer was led away for a bath, good food and new clothes. The chief baker waited nervously for his turn, hoping that Joseph had been wrong about his dream. When Pharaoh turned to him, he saw that his expression had changed, he was no longer smiling and he instructed the guard to take the baker out and hang him. The rest of the officials gasped and wondered what his crime had been. No one knew but they were all determined not to do anything that would upset Pharaoh in the future.

Three days before, when Joseph had spoken to the men about their dreams and told the cupbearer he would be released, he had asked him to speak to Pharaoh on his behalf. The position of cupbearer was a privileged one and Joseph knew that Pharaoh would listen to him. Unfortunately, his relief at being released made the cupbearer forget about his promise and it would be another two years before he remembered Joseph's request.

Once more, the time stone hummed and took the boys back to Ollie's cell.

"Why have we come back here?" demanded

Ollie, "We could have gone home!" At the sound of the cell door being unlocked, Ollie swore and picked up the bucket to give to Joseph. This, at least, was one lesson he had learned quickly. He wouldn't do anything to help himself at first but when the warder refused to come into the cell, the bucket had not been emptied for days. The stink that came from it was unbearable. Since then Ollie had made sure that he took the bucket to the door every morning. While he was handing it over, the time stone took Sam away. When Ollie turned round and saw that he was alone once more it all became too much. His bravado finally left him and he broke down in tears.

Ollie sobbed for the rest of that day, refusing to eat even the small rations that he was allowed. Eventually, exhausted from crying and in despair from being left alone once more, he lay down and fell asleep. During the night, he had a dream and in it, he saw a man in a white robe reach out his hand. The man had kind eyes and was smiling.

"Come to me," he said, "I will give you rest. Learn from me because I am gentle and humble in heart."

In his dream, Ollie reached out and took the

man's hand. As he slept a feeling of peace flowed through him.

The next morning, for the first time since he was thrown in prison, Ollie was smiling when he awoke. When Joseph arrived with bread and fresh water, Ollie asked if he knew who the man in the white robe was. Joseph smiled,

"God spoke to me last night about you. He said the man you saw was his son, whom you will meet in time. Until then I am to teach you all I know about our God."

For the next few months, Joseph taught Ollie about God who created the world and everything in it. He taught him about his sadness and anger when we are selfish and cruel and also about his great love that stops him from punishing us as we deserve. Joseph taught Ollie that the best way to live is to do as God wants and to be the best people we can be so that we honour God in everything we do.

When the time stone brought Sam back, two years later, Ollie was a very different person to the one he had left behind.

CHAPTER 10

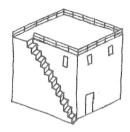

After Sam left Ollie, the time stone took him forward two years to the cell he had just left. Sam was surprised to find that Ollie looked clean and greeted him with a smile when he appeared. He smelt a lot better too!

"Er, how long is it since I was here before?" asked Sam.

"Two years," answered Ollie, "But you don't look any different."

"No, I came straight here. You are though, different I mean."

"Yes, I am. I couldn't believe it when I was left behind again. It was the worst moment of my life. Then I had a dream and Joseph told me that God wanted to help me. Joseph has visited me every day since then and taught me a lot."

"Wow, that's incredible! God answered our

prayers! I'm sure he'll let you come home now."

"You've been praying for me?"

"Every day! So have my friends back home. I told them all about you and how you were in prison."

Ollie hung his head in shame, appalled at the way he used to treat Sam when they were boys.

"I'm so sorry for the way I behaved towards you," he said.

Sam grinned, "That's okay, I forgave you ages ago. I'm just glad you've learnt how wrong it was otherwise God may never have allowed you home!"

"Is that why I'm here? To teach me a lesson?"

"No, you're here because of what you did. God would never harm us but he does use the situations we're in as an opportunity to teach us about himself. You wouldn't have come at all if you hadn't tried to kill me!"

Ollie blushed, he knew that what he had done was despicable and he finally accepted that he had only himself to blame.

"What will happen when we go home? Where will we say we've been?" Ollie asked anxiously, "My parents must have been so worried!"

"Oh, they'll never know!" laughed Sam, "We'll go back to the time we left and everything will return to how it was before. Well, almost, I'm hoping you'll still act like you are doing now!"

Ollie nodded, "I'll do my best, but what about Joseph? Won't he get into trouble if I'm no longer here?"

Sam smiled at Ollie, pleased that he finally seemed to care about someone other than himself.

"No, I'm sure he'll be fine," he said. This time, when the time stone hummed, Ollie gently held Sam's hand and with a flash of blue light, he was finally free.

It was strange being twelve again after all those years in prison. Ollie looked around, expecting to be in the park near his home.

"Where are we?" he frowned. Then, noticing his clothes he asked, "We're not still in Egypt are we?"

"No, this is first-century Bethlehem. It's the home of my friends Rachel and Matthew," laughed Sam. Ollie shook his head, rolling his eyes as he smiled,

"Well, I suppose we're closer to home than we were before!"

Leading the way to the house, Sam called a greeting when they got near to the door.

"Sam, shalom!" smiled Rachel, "Come inside. Who have you brought with you this time?"

"Rachel, this is Ollie, we've just come from the prison in Egypt."

"Oh my goodness, come, sit, you must be hungry!"

Rachel bustled about, getting bread, cheese and fruit for the boys. Matthew came in with a jug of milk, fresh that morning from Hepzibah the goat. When they were settled, Sam told the story of how Ollie had finally been set free. True to his word, Ollie remained the same as he was when Sam went back for him the last time.

"Thank you, you are very kind. I'm sure you know that I don't deserve this," Ollie said when he had eaten enough.

"Nonsense!" declared Rachel, "I know all about what happened, but I also know that Yahweh would not have brought you back if you were not ready."

"Joseph taught me a lot. I hope he didn't get into trouble when I went missing."

Rachel laughed, "Joseph became the greatest man in Egypt, second only to Pharaoh himself! It was because of him that the people had enough food to survive the drought."

Sam nodded, "His story is written in the bible. He even forgave his brothers for selling him as a slave."

"I've heard that story," said Ollie, "But I didn't realise that was the same Joseph! It's so different when you're a part of it." He shivered, "Do you think Yahweh is still angry with me?"

Rachel put her arm around him, "No, child, Yahweh loves you very much."

Matthew looked puzzled. "I wonder why he brought you here though instead of taking you home?"

Sam frowned thoughtfully. "I don't know," he said, "Although Joseph did tell Ollie that he was going to meet God's son. Every time I've met him has been with you so maybe we're going to see him before we go back."

"Who is he?" asked Ollie, "I saw him in my dream but he didn't say his name."

"It's Jesus," laughed Sam, "We've seen him loads of times, Kate and Alex have too. He's awesome."

"Well, I've heard that he is in Jerusalem for Passover," said Rachel, "There was much rejoicing when he entered the city the other day. People were singing and waving palm branches. Some even declared him king! Eli was there, he had taken some of the lambs to the temple for the celebration."

"Are we going to Jerusalem, Ima?" asked Matthew.

"We will leave tomorrow when your Abba comes back from tending the sheep. We will stay with your uncle Jacob." Rachel smiled at Sam and Ollie, "You boys can come too. Perhaps that is why you are here."

Sam nodded but a cold shiver ran down his spine. He had a feeling that this may be the last chance they had to meet Jesus. If he was right, there wouldn't be anyone singing at the end of the week.

CHAPTER 11

The walk into Jerusalem took almost two hours. The road was dry and dusty with many travellers heading into the city for the Passover celebration. Jacob welcomed them to his home and Rachel introduced Sam and Ollie as Matthew's friends. Fortunately, Jacob didn't realise Sam was the same boy he had met when Rachel was a young girl. After refreshing themselves from their journey, the three boys went for a wander around the city.

When they came to the temple they saw many people rushing about in preparation for the Passover meal to be held the next day. Lambs were an important part of the celebration and were being bought and sold in the temple courts. Matthew overheard a conversation between two of the stall-holders. Apparently, Jesus had been angry with the sellers and had overturned the tables where the money changers did business.

"I wonder why he did that?" Matthew asked, puzzled by Jesus' actions. This was one part of the bible that Sam knew well so he explained that Jesus was angry with dishonest traders who cheated their customers.

"Jesus said they had turned his house of prayer into a den of robbers," answered Sam, "The traders know the people have to buy the animals for their sacrifices so they overcharge for them."

"Oh, I see. Cheating the people is bad enough but to do it in Yahweh's house is much worse!"

The boys continued exploring, excited by the hustle and bustle of the outer court. Unlike the day when he had first travelled with Sam, Ollie stayed well away from anyone who could accuse him of doing anything wrong. A young man hurried past, almost knocking Matthew over.

"I'm sure that was Judas," he said, "Let's follow him and see if we can find Jesus."

The three boys hurried after him but stopped when they saw him enter a building attached to the north wall of the temple.

"That's the Hall of Hewn Stones," said Matthew, "It's where the Sanhedrin meet!"

"Who are they?" asked Ollie.

"They're the ones who make the rules and make sure everyone follows them. Why is Judas going there? They hate Jesus and his disciples."

As if in answer, the time stone hummed and took the boys inside the hall. Hidden behind a pillar, the boys had a good view of what was happening. Judas went up to the chief priests who led the Sanhedrin and spoke to them.

"What will you give me if I betray Jesus to you?" he asked. Counting out thirty pieces of silver, the priests laughed, delighted that they finally had a chance to get rid of the trouble maker! Matthew and Ollie were horrified as they watched one of Jesus' followers agree to give him up to the enemy. Sam just sighed, saddened by the knowledge of what was to come.

The boys were able to sneak out without being seen and they made their way back to Jacob's house. Sam warned his friends not to say anything about what they had seen.

"I know it's bad but it has to happen. I'm afraid the next few days are going to be really tough."

"Don't say any more," said Matthew, "I remember Ima saying that we shouldn't know what happens in the future. That's why we only ever go backwards in time isn't it?"

"Yes, I think so," agreed Sam.

"So, let's go in and see what there is to eat!"

The next day was Passover and the boys were kept busy helping to prepare for the evening celebration. As they worked, Matthew explained to Ollie the meaning of what they were doing.

"Passover started when Moses rescued the Israelites from Pharaoh. Each household was told to slaughter a lamb and smear its blood on the doorposts of their house. Then they had to cook and eat the lamb with unleavened bread. That's bread that doesn't need to rise so that it can be prepared quickly. The Israelites were to be packed and ready to leave as soon as Moses told them to go."

"Why put blood on the doorposts?" asked Ollie.

"It was a sign for the angel to pass over them and leave them alone, he was only allowed to enter houses that were not protected by the blood. When he did go in, he killed the firstborn son as a sign that Yahweh was more powerful than Pharaoh. Every Egyptian family was affected so Pharaoh finally gave in and let the people leave."

Sam nodded, "That was the start of their journey to Israel," he said, "and they have celebrated Passover every year since then."

"That's right, it is a reminder of what Yahweh did for us. Tonight we worship him because he rescued us from Egypt."

"Then I'm glad to be here with you," smiled Ollie, "Because he rescued me from Egypt too!"

That night, when the celebrations were over and the boys had settled down to sleep, Sam smiled as he thought about how much Ollie had changed. It was going to be a huge shock to his friends when he finally got home! Ollie must have been thinking the same thing because he rolled over to ask a question.

"Sam, I don't know what to say to Jack. He's going to think I'm so weird!"

"Yeah, he is, isn't he? I guess you'll just have to show him you're different. Dayle said it's better than telling people. If they can see you've changed they'll ask questions and then you can tell them about Jesus."

Ollie nodded, "So how do I show them, then?"

"Don't know, but I've got a feeling we're about to find out!" said Sam, taking out the stone that had begun to hum.

CHAPTER 12

They were crouched in the corner of a large room, hidden behind two huge jars of water. Next to the jars was a low table with a basin and a small pile of towels. On the far side of the room, Jesus was sat at a table with his disciples. Some women came in carrying dishes and plates and began to serve them a meal.

"That's the man I saw in my dream!" whispered Ollie.

"That's Jesus," replied Sam, "the rest are his disciples. Look, there's Judas!"

The boys watched quietly while the meal was served. Before they began to eat, Jesus stood up and came over to where the boys were hiding. Crouching lower down they tried to make themselves as small as possible. Jesus took off his outer garment and wrapped one of the towels around his waist. He didn't give any sign that he had seen the boys, he just filled the basin with water and returned to the table.

Kneeling on the floor, Jesus very gently washed and dried the feet of his disciples. Peter objected at first because it was a task for a servant but Jesus explained that he was setting them an example. He said that even though he was their Lord, he was no greater than them. If he could do this lowly task for his disciples, they could do the same for each other. He told them that they were all equal and should serve each other, just as he had served them.

"Now that you know these things," he said, "You will be blessed if you do them."

As Jesus collected up the basin and towel, the time stone hummed and took the boys back to bed.

Ollie lay quietly, thinking about what Jesus had done and said.

"I think I understand," he said, "We should treat others as though they are just as good as we are. We shouldn't act as though we are better than them."

"Yeah, it's called humility. It means we shouldn't be too proud to help those who aren't as fortunate as us."

Ollie groaned, "Sam, I'm sorry, I've been really awful haven't I?"

"Just a bit. You're not now though. I quite like the new you!"

"Do you think we can be friends when we get back?"

"Sure, why not," Sam laughed, "That will give them all something to talk about at school!"

Sam and Ollie settled down to sleep but at some time during the night, the stone took Sam away.

He was on a hillside outside the city, in a garden, lying near to the disciples. They were all fast asleep. A commotion near the entrance woke Sam, who was surprised that he was no longer in bed. Jesus hurried over and woke the disciples.

"Are you still sleeping?" he asked, "Look, the hour is near, and the Son of Man is betrayed into the hands of sinners. Rise, let us go! Here comes my betrayer!"

The disciples stood up, confused because they had only just woken up. Sam realised what was about to happen and he slipped quietly behind a bush, where he could watch without being seen. A large crowd had arrived, armed with swords and clubs. Amongst them was Judas, who approached Jesus and kissed him on the cheek. This was the signal for the men to arrest him. Jesus stood calmly, allowing them to do what they had come for.

One of the disciples drew his sword, to try to defend his Lord. They were upset, especially when they saw that it was one of their group who had betrayed him. He struck the high priest's servant, cutting off his ear, but Jesus admonished him saying, "No more of this!" Then Jesus touched the man and healed him.

The crowd led Jesus away but the disciples were afraid and they all scattered in different directions. Sam wasn't sure what to do so he followed Peter who was walking quickly, a little way behind the crowd. When they came to the high priest's house, the leaders took Jesus inside while the rest kept warm around a fire in the courtyard. Peter joined them as though he had been one of the crowd, he was waiting to see what would happen. Sam sat nearby, not wanting to get too close.

One of the group looked closely at Peter, "This man was with him," she said. Peter denied it but a while later someone else said the same thing.

Peter denied it again but the others kept looking at him, unsure if they believed him. Eventually, a third person spoke up, declaring that Peter was one of Jesus' followers.

Peter became angry and swore saying, "Man, I don't know what you're talking about!" A cock crowed to greet the morning and inside the house, Jesus turned and looked through a window, straight at Peter. Then Peter remembered what Jesus had told him at the Passover meal the evening before.

"Before the cock crows today, you will disown me three times."

Ashamed at what he had done, Peter ran out of the courtyard and wept bitterly. Sam felt sorry for Peter, the crowd that had come for Jesus had been violent and the disciples were no match for them. He thought it had been brave of Peter to follow them but he wasn't at all surprised that he couldn't admit to knowing Jesus. Who knew what would have happened to him if he had!

Not long after, the chief priests and other members of the Sanhedrin bound Jesus tightly and led him out. They took him to be questioned by Pilate, who was the governor of Jerusalem. Sam followed them, being careful to avoid being seen.

Outside the house, a crowd had gathered. Sam recognised some of them from the crowd that had arrested Jesus in the garden. Pilate brought Jesus out onto the balcony. At that time it was the custom for a prisoner to be released at the Passover Feast so, speaking to the crowd, he asked,

"Do you want me to release the one you call the king of the Jews?"

But the crowd had been stirred up by the chief priests so they replied, "Release Barabbas!" Barabbas had been accused of murder and of causing a riot against the government, the same crime that the chief priests were accusing Jesus of. Even though Jesus was innocent, the people asked for the guilty Barabbas to be set free instead. Then, when Pilate asked what he should do with Jesus, they replied,

"Crucify him!"

Sam stood on the edge of the crowd, a look of anguish on his face. He knew this had to happen, but he was shocked by the response of the people. They even cheered when Pilate agreed to their demand!

Not wanting to see any more, Sam went back to Jacob's house saddened by all that had happened.

◆ ◆ ◆

"Sam, where have you been?" asked Rachel, "We have been so worried!"

Sam realised that for once, the time stone was working in real-time and had only moved him to a different location. He asked Rachel, Matthew and Ollie to join him outside, out of hearing from the others. When he told them everything he had seen, Matthew became angry with the disciples.

"Why did they run away and why was Peter such a coward?" he demanded.

"Hush, Matthew! We don't know what it was like for them," said Rachel, who thought that they were probably terrified.

Sam nodded, "It was awful, but I do think Jesus understood. The way that he looked at Peter was sad but he didn't look angry. It's no wonder Peter was upset when he realised what he had done."

"So what happens now?" asked Ollie.

"They will make him carry his cross through the streets to Golgotha where they will nail him to it," whispered Rachel, tears streaming down her face, "Then they will raise it and leave him there until he dies!"

The three boys looked horrified. How cruel

could people be? Even the guilty didn't deserve to die like that!

"Come, let us ask Yahweh to save his son," suggested Rachel. The boys agreed but Sam and Ollie both knew that he wouldn't. Everything that was happening now was the reason they celebrated Easter in the twenty-first century. The four friends joined hands and bowed their heads in prayer. As they did so, the time stone hummed and even though none of them wanted to see Jesus die, it took them to the hill where three crosses stood, each bearing a man found guilty.

Sam could see Peter, standing a little further away. His head hung in shame and he sobbed at the sight of his Lord and friend hanging on the cross. Sam wanted to go up to him to tell him that Jesus loved him and would forgive him but wasn't sure if he should. He moved a few steps closer, thinking that he could just stand near him when the time stone hummed and whisked him away.

CHAPTER 13

It was a shock to be back on the dunes behind the cottage. Sam couldn't believe that he had come home from such an important time in history. All thoughts of ringing home forgotten, Sam turned round and went back to find his friends.

"Back so soon, Sam?" asked Sue, "Could you not get through to your mum?"

"Didn't try, I've been back to Israel!"

As soon as he said this, the others crowded round to hear the latest chapter in the story.

"Have you seen Ollie?" asked Kate.

"How is he?" Ben wanted to know.

"Where is he?" frowned Alex as though he expected him to jump out from behind the dunes.

"Yes, I've seen him, he's fine and he's in Jerusalem with Rachel," answered Sam, "But ...." Sam frowned, bit his lip and closed his eyes tightly. He could still see Jesus on the cross and tears began to trickle down his cheeks. He shook his head and sat down, hugging his knees to try to reconnect with where he was now. It wasn't easy as his thoughts were still very much on a hill in Jerusalem.

Taking a deep breath, he poured out his story from when he first went back to see Ollie get arrested in Egypt.

"Oh, Sam," said Sue sadly, putting her arms around him when he got to the end. No one else said a word. The thought of seeing Jesus on the cross was more than any of them could bear. Quietly they all linked hands, each one thinking of all the things they had to say sorry for and thanking Jesus that he had died for them so that they could be forgiven. As they each joined together with Sam, the time stone hummed and took them all to Golgotha.

Chris, Sue, Dayle and Jamie gasped when they realised that they had travelled back to the first century. Any doubts they may have had before were instantly dispelled when they had recovered enough to look around. Chris stroked his face, he'd even grown a beard! Alex, Ben and Kate, now seasoned time travellers, smiled sadly at the four first-timers. This was a very different trip to any other they had been on. Standing before the cross, they all saw how much Jesus had suffered because of their wrongdoing. They realised how much God must love them to allow his son to sacrifice himself for them in this way.

Sam sighed and left his friends to go and look for Rachel. She wasn't far away, still standing in the place he had left her. Matthew and Ollie were on either side, comforting her as she cried at the sight in front of her. Jesus' mother, Mary, stood at the foot of the cross with John, Peter stood to one side and the other disciples were scattered amongst the crowd.

Although it was still early afternoon, the sun stopped shining and everywhere was darker than night. Not even the stars twinkled in the sky. Sam shivered, it was cold without the sun. Those who had mocked and insulted Jesus muttered quietly as the darkness continued. Even the birds were silent. Then, after three hours, Jesus cried out,

"My God, my God, why have you forsaken me?"

Someone held up a stick with a sponge on the end soaked in vinegar. Jesus drank a little from it, then, in a loud voice, he said, "It is finished."

An earthquake shook the city and the curtain in the temple was torn in two. Jesus, the Son of God, was dead.

After a few minutes, Rachel wiped her eyes and sighed. "Come, there is nothing more to be done. His friends will care for his body. We must prepare for the Sabbath."

"Er, Rachel," Sam hesitated, not sure that this was the best time to introduce more of his friends from the twenty-first century.

Rachel smiled sadly, "Don't worry Sam, I saw them arrive. They are welcome to join us."

Sam sighed with relief and turned to introduce the four newcomers who had come looking for Sam. Ollie stepped back, not sure how well he would be received. As if in answer, Alex went up to him and held out his hand.

"Shalom," he smiled, "Sam has told us all about your time in Egypt. I'm glad you're here."

"Shalom, and thank you." Ollie said as he shook hands with Alex, "I'm sorry for the trouble I've caused."

"That's okay," grinned Alex, "I'm looking forward to going back to school and seeing everyone's faces when you and Sam turn up as friends!"

"Yeah, that's what Sam said!" Ollie grinned

sheepishly, relieved that Sam's friends had accepted him.

Chris and Sue walked ahead with Rachel, chatting quietly. They told her how pleased they were to meet her after all the help she had given to Sam. When Rachel realised that Chris was Sam's rabbi she was surprised at how young he was.

"Most of our rabbis are old men!" she exclaimed. They laughed, relaxing a little as they began to put the last few hours behind them. Even so, the small group of friends remained subdued when they got back to Jacob's and had to tell them all that had happened that day.

Space was found for the extra guests and during the rest of the evening and throughout the Sabbath the following day, they shared stories of the times they had met Jesus. Their favourite was when Sam had asked him to heal Eli's wife and he had stopped off to see her on his way to Jerusalem. They had all thought Dinah wouldn't live but the day after Jesus' visit she was up sweeping the courtyard and singing praise to God!

It had been good to share their memories but

Rachel and Matthew were still struggling to come to terms with the death of the one they believed to be their Messiah. The nine travellers from the future found it hard to keep quiet when they saw how sad their friends were. They knew that they couldn't say anything about what the next day would bring, even though it was the most wonderful thing to happen in the whole of history!

CHAPTER 14

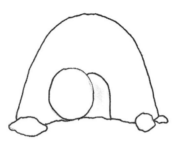

On Sunday morning, Sam and his friends got up early, grinning excitedly. They couldn't wait any longer, they knew that from now on, everything was going to change! Rachel was in the kitchen, putting fruit on the table for breakfast. Her eyes were red and swollen from crying and she was not pleased when she saw Sam.

"How can you be so happy?" she asked, "Jesus is dead, what are we to do now?"

Sue put her arms around the older woman and hugged her. "Come with us," she said, "We have something wonderful to show you."

They each took some fruit from the basket and led Rachel outside to where Matthew was collecting eggs from the hens.

"Where are we going?" she asked.

"To the tomb where they put Jesus," replied Sam,

"Do you know the way?"

"Yes, of course, but the women will be preparing his body with spices. They won't want us there."

"Trust us," said Chris, "You must come and see."

Rachel sighed and pursed her lips. Did they not understand what this meant for her nation?

Grumbling quietly, Rachel reluctantly showed them the way to the tombs which were outside the city. Before they got there, however, they saw a man in a white robe walking towards them. As they got closer they could see that he was smiling.

"Why is everyone so happy?" demanded Rachel crossly.

The man reached out and took her by the hand, "Rachel," he said gently, "They are happy because I am alive!"

Rachel and Matthew both gasped when they realised that the man was Jesus!

"Oh, my goodness!" exclaimed Rachel as her knees gave way. Jesus caught her before she fell and hugged her close. Tears of joy streamed down her face, replacing the sorrow that had over-whelmed her. Matthew looked at the group of friends who were all grinning like Cheshire cats.

"You knew!" he said, amazed that they had kept it secret.

"Yes, I'm sorry," said Sam, "We wanted to tell you but we knew we couldn't."

Matthew shook his head, speechless at seeing Jesus standing before him, no longer dead but well and truly alive!

Jesus walked with them back towards the city, quietly speaking to each of them in turn. Drawing Sam aside, he asked if he had enjoyed his time travel journey.

"Not all of it!" he admitted, "Some bits were quite scary."

Jesus nodded, "Yes, but I was always with you, I would never leave you to go through it alone."

"I know that now. Thank you for being with me, I've learnt so much." Sam frowned, "Will I be able to come back? I'm sure there's a lot more I need to know!"

"Oh Sam, there is so much more!" Jesus looked at him thoughtfully, "Perhaps you can, I will ask my Father when I return to him. For now, you have work to do in your own time. You must tell others about me and both Ollie and Ben are going to need your friendship."

Sam nodded, "I would like to say goodbye to Rachel and Matthew."

Jesus smiled, "Well, maybe just 'au revoir' for now! In the meantime, I am going to take Ollie home. Things are not quite as you left them."

Sam watched Jesus speak to Ollie, puzzled by his last words. He shrugged and caught up with Rachel and Matthew.

"Oh, Sam, isn't it wonderful! We are going home to tell everyone!" Rachel laughed, all her sorrow had disappeared and she reminded Sam of the young girl had first met on the hillside outside Bethlehem.

Sam grinned, "We're going home too. I asked if I would come back but Jesus wouldn't say. He told me to say 'au revoir' though. It means until we meet again."

"Then may it be so. Until then, shalom! I have enjoyed our journey." Rachel hugged Sam for the last time and walked quickly towards Jerusalem, singing and praising God.

Sam gathered his friends together so that they could join hands and as they did so, the time stone began to hum.

"But what about Ollie?" asked Kate, panicking

that he would be left behind again.

"It's okay," smiled Sam, "He's with Jesus!"

Back on the beach behind the cottage, the group collected up their belongings then went home to celebrate with barbecued sausages and ice cream.

"And chocolate!" shouted Kate, "We always have chocolate at Easter!"

EPILOGUE

The rest of the holiday was spent surfing and playing games with a boat trip on the broads and a walk to see the seals at Waxham. When they returned home to their parents, they declared it had been the best holiday ever.

Although Sam kept the time stone nearby it remained silent and the rest of the summer was spent helping out with his grandparents and meeting up with whichever members of the group were around. Thankfully, his gran was soon able to care for herself but not soon enough to allow them to go back to the cottage. Sam didn't mind, the two weeks he'd had with his friends was worth the whole of the summer on his own.

It wasn't until the five friends met up in the park the week after they got back that they finally found out what had happened to Ollie. His friend Jack was at the hospital having the cast removed from his foot so Ollie was alone, throwing stones into the lake just like the day when he had attacked Sam and been transported back in time to Egypt.

"Hey, Ollie!" called Sam, running up to him, "We've all been wondering what happened to you!"

"Oh, hello!" Ollie dropped the stones he was holding and they sat down on the grass to hear his story.

"I had a long chat with Jesus before I got back. I told him how sorry I was for all the stuff I'd done, not just here but in Egypt too."

"What did he say?" asked Jamie, while Ben just smiled and nodded, he'd had a similar conversation with Jesus too.

"Most of it was about how much he loved me and that he understood. But he also talked about Dad and how I could help him."

"Your Dad? Why?" Sam was curious, he hadn't known there was a problem.

Ollie explained about his father's time in the army and how he had been selected for the pentathlon until a fall from his horse had left him disabled. His frustrations at having to give it all up had led him to gambling, drinking and taking it out on Ollie.

"Oh, poor you," whispered Kate, horrified at Ollie's story.

"But how can you help?" asked Alex.

Ollie sighed, "I didn't get back until the day after I attacked Sam and the time stone took us to Egypt. I'd been missing for a whole day and night."

"Oh wow, what did you tell them when you got home?" asked Sam, shocked that Ollie was missing for twenty-four hours, "Were they worried?"

"Oh yeah, the police were there at the house!"

The others gasped, they hadn't expected this!

"I told them I'd spent the night in the park. Mum was frantic, she thought I'd been murdered!"

"What about your Dad?" asked Ben, "Was he angry?"

"No, he was really quiet. I think he realised he was to blame, especially after he'd told the police we'd had a fight. They were acting really suspicious, it sounded like they thought he'd done something to me. Anyway, after the police had gone he asked me why I hadn't come home. Jesus had told me to be as honest as I could so I told him I was fed up with him bullying me to do better at sports all the time. Then I said that he needed to get help for his problems. I told him I couldn't win his medals for him and he should get himself fit for the Invictus Games."

Ben's eyes nearly popped out on stalks, he wouldn't dream of speaking to his father like that! Sam just nodded, no wonder Jesus had told him to be a friend to Ollie!

"Did your Dad listen to you?" asked Kate.

"Yeah, he did," nodded Ollie, "I was gobsmacked! I thought he would hit the roof but I think he was scared something had happened to me and the police would blame him. Anyway, he's going to see a counsellor so maybe things will start to get better."

"You won't give up your sports though will you? You're too good!" declared Alex.

"No, but it won't take over like it did before."

"Maybe you could help your Dad to train, you know, for the Invictus Games," suggested Jamie.

Ollie grinned at the thought, "Yeah, maybe."

The six friends spent the afternoon chatting about their adventures before making their separate ways home.

Sam smiled, he was looking forward to Year eight and he was especially looking forward to the reactions of his class when he and Ollie turned up together!

Yeah, he thought, the next year promised to be a very different experience altogether!

PASSOVER SEDER

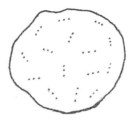

The *Passover Seder* is a celebration meal held on Maundy Thursday, to remember the night of the final plague that persuaded Pharaoh to set the Israelites free. It is very important to the Jewish people and was the last meal that Jesus shared with his disciples before his arrest. During the meal, certain things are said and done so that the Israelites would never forget how God saved them from slavery and brought them out of Egypt to the Promised Land.

Seder means the order and content of the celebration and the words and blessings spoken are read from the *Haggadah* which means text.

Candles are lit by a woman or an older girl while she speaks a blessing.

Parsley dipped in saltwater represents life and the tears shed by the slaves.

A *bitter herb*, such as *horseradish* or *romaine let-*

tuce, represents the hard work of the slaves. It is usually eaten with *charoset,* a sweet paste made of apples and nuts which represents the mortar used by the slaves for building.

Unleavened bread, flatbread made without yeast, represents the need for haste. The Israelites needed to be packed and ready to leave as soon as Pharaoh said go so there was no time to wait for the yeast to work.

Lamb, roasted or made into a stew, represents the sacrifice made by the lamb which set their homes apart from the Egyptians. The lamb's blood was smeared onto the door frame to show the angel that they were protected by God and he was not allowed to enter to take their first-born sons.

Wine or *grape juice* is drunk to represent God's promises of redemption and acceptance.

During the meal, the Passover story is read from the book of Exodus and prayers and blessings are spoken. Songs are also sung making it a joyful celebration of remembrance, thanks and praise.

MODERN PASSOVER RECIPES

Charoset

4 apples	½ cup nuts	½ tsp cinnamon
2 tbsp sugar	2 tbsp grape juice	

Chop nuts and apples (a food processor will help)
Mix with sugar and cinnamon   Moisten with juice.

Passover Rolls

4 eggs	2 cups matzo meal
1 tsp salt	1 tbsp sugar
1 cup water	½ cup oil

Mix matzo meal, salt and sugar in a bowl
Boil water and oil in a saucepan,
pour onto matzo meal, mix well
Add eggs, one at a time
Shape into 12 balls, place on a greased baking sheet
Bake 45 mins until brown - 375 F / 190 C / mk 5

Potato Latkes

6 medium potatoes grated   1 cup grated onion
½ cup grated carrot   ¼ cup matzo meal
1 ½ tsp salt   ¼ tsp pepper   4 egg whites

Mix all ingredients
Place ¼ cup of mixture into greased muffin tray
Bake 45 min - 375 F / 190 C / mk 5
Tip out onto a baking sheet
Bake for a further 10 min until crisp
Serve with apple sauce and sour cream
Makes about 24

THE INVICTUS GAMES

The first Invictus Games happened in London in 2014. They were started by Prince Harry who had been a captain in the British army. He had attended the Warrior Games in the USA and discovered how sport was able to help those who suffered from injuries and illness.

Invictus means **unconquerable** and the games are for men and women in the armed forces who have been injured while serving their country. Just like the Paralympics, some contestants have lost arms or legs and compete with the aid of wheelchairs or artificial limbs.

The games are held every year (although they had a break for covid) in countries all around the world.

In April 2022, 500 competitors from 20 nations competed in The Hague on the southwest coast of The Netherlands.

If you want to find out more, visit their website …

www.invictusgamesfoundation.org

Don't forget to check with your responsible adult first!

BIBLE REFERENCES

If you would like to read about the events and places that Sam visited, you will find them in the Christian bible. There are lots of different translations but one of the easiest to understand is the Good News Bible.

Old Testament Stories

God speaks to Moses - *Exodus ch 3 vs 1 – 6*
Battle of Jericho - *Joshua ch 5 vs 13 – ch 6 vs 20*
Joseph - *Genesis ch 39 vs 20 – ch 40 vs 23*

New Testament Stories

Archangel Michael - *Revelation ch 12 vs 7*
Angel speaks to John - *Revelation ch 22 vs 8 - 9*
Simeon & Anna in the temple - *Luke ch 2 vs 22 – 38*
Joseph and Mary warned - *Matthew ch 2 vs 13 – 23*
The house on the rock - *Matthew ch 7 vs 24 – 27*
"Come to me…" - *Matthew ch 11 vs 28 – 29*
Commander - *Revelation ch 19 vs 11 - 16*

Jesus' Final Week

Entry into Jerusalem - *Matthew ch 21 vs 1 – 11*
Anger at the traders - *Mark ch 11 vs 15 – 18*
Judas' betrayal - *Matthew ch 26 vs 14 – 16*
Foot washing - *John ch 13 vs 1 – 17*
Arrest - *Luke ch 22 vs 47 - 53*
Peter's denial - *Luke ch 22 vs 54 – 62*
Before Pilate - *Mark ch 15 vs 1 – 15*
Crucifixion - *John ch 19 vs 28 – 37*
Resurrection - *Matthew ch 28 vs 1 – 10*

AFTERWORD

Sam learnt a lot about God during his trips into the past. He learnt that God is faithful and kind and loves us all very much. But he also learned that God wants us to love him and give him the respect and honour that he deserves. After all, he is the one who created us!

If you want to know more about God who made the world and about his Son, Jesus, you can read all about him in the Christian bible. But the best way to get to know him is to ask him to be your friend.

Jesus died on the cross for YOU so that you can be forgiven for all the bad stuff that you've done. (Don't worry, everyone does stuff they shouldn't, including me!)

The amazing thing though is that he didn't stay dead! When Jesus came back to life it meant that one day, when it's our turn, we will come back to life too and live with him in Heaven. Isn't that awesome!

If you would like Jesus to be your friend and help you to be the best person you can be, why not say the prayer that's written here.

Dear Jesus

Thank you that you came to earth to teach me how to live the best life. I'm sorry for the times I get it wrong. Please forgive me.

Thank you for giving your life for me. I know you love me. I love you too.

I believe you are God's Son and that you want to be my friend. I want to be your friend too.

Amen

GLOSSARY

Abba - *Dad, daddy*

Aghast - *shocked, horrified*

Admonish - *warn, tell off*

Anguish - *extremely distressed*

Apprentice - *one who learns a trade*

Archangel - *angel of high rank*

Bravado - *being bold to impress others*

Chaperone - *responsible companion*

Crucify - *Roman form of execution*

Custom - *accepted way of doing something*

Disciples - *students*

Discredit - *destroy someone's reputation*

Dispel - *make something go away*

Disown - *refuse to have anymore to do with*

Distraught - *very worried and upset*

Erosion - *wearing away*

Exodus - *mass departure of people*

Expertise - *skill*

Fervently - *intensely enthusiastic*

Forsaken - *abandoned, deserted*

Gentile - *non-Jewish person*

Ima - *Mum, mummy*

Incredulous - *unwilling to believe something*

Invictus - *unconquerable*

Manna - *food from heaven*

Meagre - *small amount, inadequate*

Messiah - *Saviour*

Overwhelmed - *too much of something*

Passover - *celebration to remember the Exodus*

Proclaim - *declare emphatically*

Rabbi – *teacher*

Redemption - *saved from sin or suffering*

Sacred - *dedicated to God, holy*

Sacrifice - *offering of extreme value*

Sanhedrin - *supreme council*

Sceptical - *doubting*

Shalom - *peace, often said as a greeting*

Subdued - *quiet, reflective or depressed*

Understatement - *saying something is less than it is*

Unkempt - *untidy, dishevelled*

THANK YOU!

Thanks as ever to all those who have encouraged and supported me during Sam's journey. It has been as much mine as his and every prayer and kind word have been much appreciated.

Praise and thanks always to Jesus. He has been by my side every step of the way.

Thank you for sticking with me, I hope you have enjoyed the journey as much as I have!

ABOUT THE AUTHOR

Gill Parkes

Gill lives in Norfolk with her husband where she enjoys walks along the beach and exploring the countryside. She loves to spend time with her grandchildren, especially snuggling up to share a good book.

She started to write about Sam's journey when God asked her to teach the children about him. She thought she might manage just one or two books so it was a shock when God said to write a rainbow! Now here we are with number seven, the rainbow's complete, but there is still much more to learn!

Sam asked, "Will I be able to come back? I'm sure there's a lot more I need to know!"

Well, only God knows the answer to that but for now, "Au revoir," until we meet again!

PRAISE FOR AUTHOR

'Expertly written and full of scriptural knowledge and context, Gill Parkes has produced a valuable series of books for children that can be enjoyed by all ages and which skilfully and lovingly open up not just a world of exciting adventure but also the world of truth that is faith in Jesus Christ.'

- JAMES MACINTYRE
JOURNALIST AND AUTHOR

SAM PARROW'S TIME TRAVEL ADVENTURES

Sam travels through time to learn about God, how much he is loved and his own special place in God's world.

Sam Parrow And The Time Stone To Bethlehem

Sam Parrow Back In Time For Dinner

Sam Parrow And The Time Stone Secret

Sam Parrow In Time To Save A Dodo

Sam Parrow Back When Time Stood Still

Sam Parrow Stuck In Time

Sam Parrow Time To Say Goodbye

"Jesus did many other things as well. If every one of them were written down, I suppose that even the whole world would not have room for the books that would be written."

John ch 21 vs 25

Printed in Great Britain
by Amazon

78280743R00068